ANIMALS UNDERCOVER
CAMOUFLAGE

Gareth Stevens
PUBLISHING

BY MADELEINE FORTESCUE << <<

Please visit our website, www.garethstevens.com. For a free color catalog of all our high-quality books, call toll free 1-800-542-2595 or fax 1-877-542-2596.

Library of Congress Cataloging-in-Publication Data

Fortescue, Madeleine, author.
 Animals undercover : camouflage / Madeleine Fortescue.
    pages cm. — (Ultimate animal defenses)
 Includes bibliographical references and index.
 ISBN 978-1-4824-4441-4 (pbk.)
 ISBN 978-1-4824-4385-1 (6 pack)
 ISBN 978-1-4824-4423-0 (library binding)
 1. Camouflage (Biology)—Juvenile literature. 2. Protective coloration (Biology)—Juvenile literature. 3. Animals—Color—Juvenile literature. 4. Animal behavior—Juvenile literature. I. Title.
 QL767.F67 2017
 591.47′2—dc23

                            2015021481

First Edition

Published in 2017 by
Gareth Stevens Publishing
111 East 14th Street, Suite 349
New York, NY 10003

Copyright © 2017 Gareth Stevens Publishing

Designer: Katelyn E. Reynolds
Editor: Therese Shea

Photo credits: Cover, p. 1 Ryan M. Bolton/Shutterstock.com; cover, pp. 1–24 (background texture) vector illustration/Shutterstock.com; p. 5 Ajayptp/Shutterstock.com; p. 7 (main) Barry Blackburn/ Shutterstock.com; p. 7 (inset) Nagel Photography/Shutterstock.com; p. 9 Art Wolfe/The Image Bank/ Getty Images; p. 11 2630ben/Shutterstock.com; p. 13 (butterfly) Agustin Esmoris/Shutterstock.com; p. 13 (butterflyfish) Chris Huss/Florida Keys National Marine Sanctuary/Wikipedia.org; p. 13 (peacock) Chase Clausen/Shutterstock.com; p. 13 (crab) Wild Horizons/UIG via Getty Images; p. 13 (hawk moth) Dimijian Greg/Science Source/Getty Images; p. 13 (serval) Kitch Bain/Shutterstock.com; p. 15 kwest/ Shutterstock.com; p. 16 Johan Larson/Shutterstock.com; p. 17 Barcroft Media/Getty Images; p. 19 (left) Laurie Campbell/The Image Bank/Getty Images; p. 19 (right) Paul Nicklen/National Geographic/Getty Images; p. 21 Dario Sabljak/Shutterstock.com.

Printed in the United States of America

CPSIA compliance information: Batch #CS16GS : For further information contact Gareth Stevens, New York, New York at 1-800-542-2595.

CONTENTS

Out of Nowhere.. 4

Camouflaged by Color.. 6

Can You Spot It?.. 8

All Together Now 10

Copycat!.. 12

Undercover Underwater... 14

Insects in Disguise 16

Changing with the Seasons.................................... 18

The Best Tricks of All?... 20

Glossary.. 22

For More Information 23

Index.. 24

Words in the glossary appear in **bold** type the first time they are used in the text.

OUT OF NOWHERE

Have you ever been on a walk through the woods or in a park when an animal seemed to come out of nowhere? Perhaps a snake or toad just seemed to appear under your feet or on a path. These creatures didn't just magically pop into place. They likely had a body colored to help them blend in with the **environment**. You didn't see them until they moved.

This coloring is called camouflage. Camouflage can also be an animal's shape or even movement. It's an important **adaptation** that many kinds of animals have.

CAMOUFLAGED BY COLOR

Many **mammals** have fur that blends in with their environment. For example, gray squirrels have fur that's a mix of white, black, and brown. It's also a bit uneven. So, from a distance, the squirrel is hard to see next to tree bark. A squirrel's fur helps it hide from predators, including hawks and owls.

Polar bear fur looks white, helping the bears blend in with their snowy, icy **habitat**. Polar bears don't need to worry about predators. They're at the top of their food chain. However, their coloring helps them surprise their prey: seals.

CAN YOU THINK OF ANY OTHER MAMMALS WITH FUR THAT CAMOUFLAGES THEM?

SO WILD!

Polar bears actually have black skin. They appear white because their see-through hairs shine back light the way snow and ice do. Otherwise they'd be easy to spot in the snow!

7

CAN YOU SPOT IT?

A cheetah is famous for its spotted coat. However, in its own habitat, this **pattern** is actually a kind of camouflage.

Cheetahs make their home in the grasslands of Africa and Iran. They hunt during the day when the sun shines on the grasses and creates shadows. The cheetah's spotted coat helps it blend in with both the yellow grasses and the dark shadows. It can stay hidden from both prey, such as gazelles, and predators, such as lions.

SO WILD!

A tiger's stripes also help it hide in the shadows of grasslands and forests.

9

ALL TOGETHER NOW

A zebra's black and white stripes might seem to stand out in its African habitat. Scientists wondered for years why zebras have this special coat. Today, many think it's a kind of camouflage to guard zebras from predators.

Lions like to pick out a single zebra to attack. However, when they approach a whole herd of zebras, the many black and white stripes in the group may confuse, or mix up, the predators. The **color-blind** lions can't pick out just one zebra—the herd looks like a jumble of stripes!

SO WILD!

Each zebra has a **unique** pattern of stripes. This may help zebras tell each other apart!

ANOTHER NAME FOR A ZEBRA'S
KIND OF CAMOUFLAGE IS
DISRUPTIVE COLORATION.

COPYCAT!

Mimicry (MIH-mihk-ree) is when an animal copies the appearance, actions, or sounds of another animal. For example, many animals have eyespots on their body, which are large circular spots that look like the eyes of much larger animals.

Some animals have coloring or markings that make them look like poisonous or bad-tasting animals that predators are less likely to eat. The harmless scarlet king snake looks a lot like the poisonous coral snake. The robber fly even makes noises similar to a more dangerous animal—the bumblebee!

SPOT THE EYESPOT

owl butterfly

foureye butterflyfish

peacock

ANIMALS THAT USE EYESPOT MIMICRY

ocellate swimming crab

hawk moth

serval

13

UNDERCOVER UNDERWATER

Did you ever wonder why penguins have a white stomach? Scientists think this is a kind of camouflage called countershading. Countershaded animals have different colors on their back and stomach.

Penguins spend much of their life in the water. Predators swimming below a penguin—such as sharks, seals, and killer whales—may not be able to see it because its white stomach blends in with sunlight. Predators swimming above the penguin may have a hard time seeing it, too. A penguin's black back is camouflaged to look like the dark waters beneath it.

SO WILD!

Some birds, dolphins, and fish also have countershading.

INSECTS IN DISGUISE

Some kinds of **insects** are masters of **disguise**. Most species, or kinds, of katydids look like green leaves, which is handy since they live in trees, grasses, and bushes.

Walkingsticks are green or brown insects that truly look like sticks. They even walk in a way that makes them appear like sticks being blown by the wind.

There are about 1,500 species of mantises. Some look like green leaves, others like dead leaves, and some like beautiful flowers!

CHANGING WITH THE SEASONS

Most animals have some kind of camouflage, but some animals have an even better trick: They can change their coloring to match their changing environment. Arctic **hares** have beautiful white or blue-gray coats that act as camouflage in their snowy winter habitat. In the spring, when the snow melts, the hare sheds, or loses, its coat and grows brown or gray fur that matches the rocky environment.

An Arctic fox's coat changes with the seasons, too. These animals use their camouflage to try to surprise their prey—Arctic hares!

SO WILD!

In the winter, Arctic hares may live in groups of hundreds or thousands!

THE BEST TRICKS OF ALL?

Other animals have tricky camouflage adaptations, too. The California ground squirrel uses a camouflage smell! It chews up rattlesnake skin and spits it on its bushy tail. When a rattlesnake smells the skin, it's confused. It thinks the squirrel might be a rattlesnake.

Octopuses can change colors to match their environment perfectly—even though they're color-blind! They can also change the **texture** of their skin so it looks bumpy, smooth, or spiky, just like objects on the ocean floor.

What's your favorite kind of animal camouflage?

SO WILD!

Lizards called chameleons are famous for turning colors. However, scientists aren't sure whether a chameleon changes color for camouflage or for other reasons.

GLOSSARY

adaptation: a change in a type of animal that makes it better able to live in its surroundings

color-blind: unable to see the difference between colors

disguise: a changed appearance so that something or someone's true form can't be known

disruptive: thrown into disorder or broken apart

environment: the conditions that surround a living thing and affect the way it lives

habitat: the natural place where an animal or plant lives

hare: a fast animal that looks like a large rabbit but has longer ears and legs

insect: a small, often winged, animal with six legs and three body parts

mammal: a warm-blooded animal that has a backbone and hair, breathes air, and feeds milk to its young

pattern: the way colors or shapes happen over and over again

texture: the way something feels when touched

unique: one of a kind

FOR MORE INFORMATION

BOOKS

Irwin, Bindi, with Chris Kunz. *Camouflage*. Naperville, IL: Sourcebooks Jabberwocky, 2011.

Stevenson, Emma. *Hide-and-Seek Science: Animal Camouflage*. New York, NY: Holiday House, 2013.

Yaw, Valerie. *Color-Changing Animals*. New York, NY: Bearport Publishing, 2011.

WEBSITES

Camouflage
education.nationalgeographic.com/education/encyclopedia/camouflage/
Check out the amazing camouflage photos on this site.

How Animal Camouflage Works
animals.howstuffworks.com/animal-facts/animal-camouflage.htm
Read more about different kinds of camouflage.

INDEX

Arctic fox 18

Arctic hares 18, 19

cheetah 8, 9

coat 8, 9, 10, 18

color 4, 6, 12, 18, 20, 21

countershading 14, 15

disguise 16

disruptive coloration 11

eyespots 12, 13

fur 6, 7

insects 16

katydids 16

mammals 6

mantises 16, 17

mimicry 12, 13

octopuses 20, 21

pattern 8

penguins 14

polar bears 6, 7, 19

skin 7, 20

smell 20

squirrels 6, 20

texture 20

walkingsticks 16

zebras 10, 11